IN THE NIGHT KITCHEN

MAURICE SENDAK

THE BODLEY HEAD, LONDON

ISBN 0 370 01549 5
COPYRIGHT © 1970 BY MAURICE SENDAK
LETTERING BY DIANA BLAIR
FIRST PUBLISHED IN GREAT BRITAIN 1971
PRINTED BY WILLIAM CLOWES & SONS, BECCLES

 FOR SADIE AND PHILIP

AND THEY PUT THAT BATTER UP TO BAKE

A DELICIOUS MICKEY-CAKE.

SO HE SKIPPED FROM THE OVEN & INTO BREAD DOUGH ALL READY TO RISE IN THE NIGHT KITCHEN.

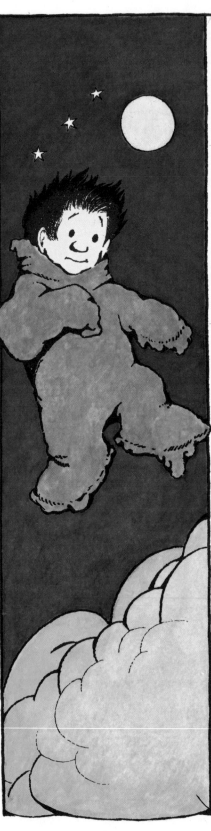

TILL IT LOOKED OKAY.

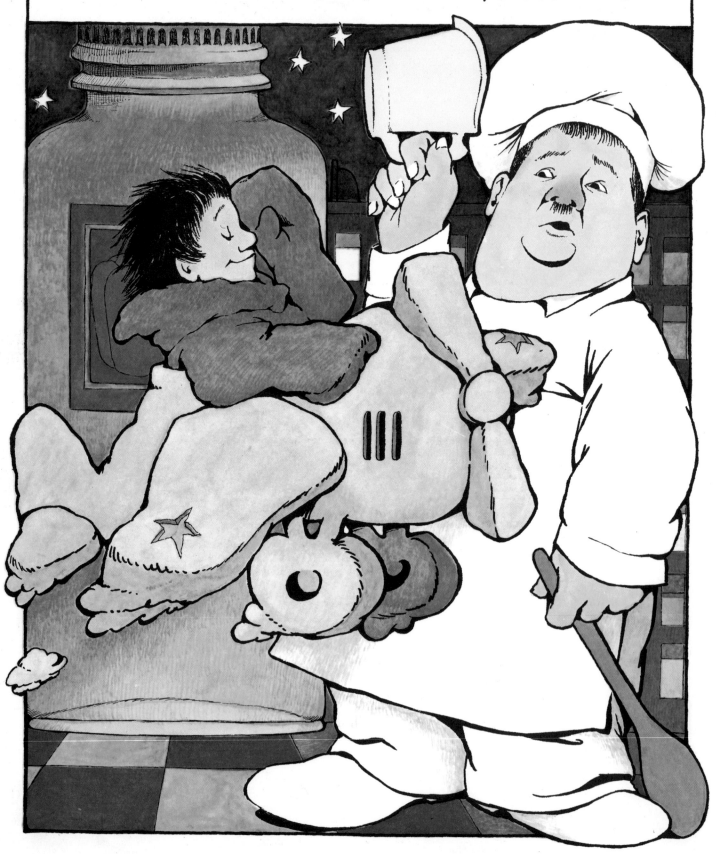

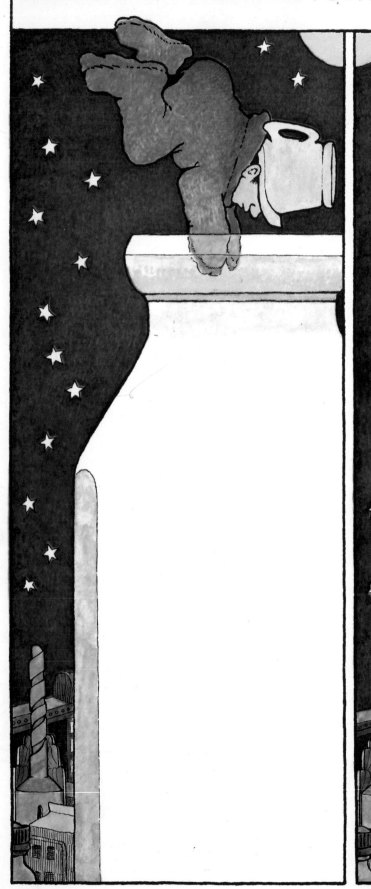

SO THE BAKERS THEY MIXED IT AND BEAT IT AND BAKED IT.

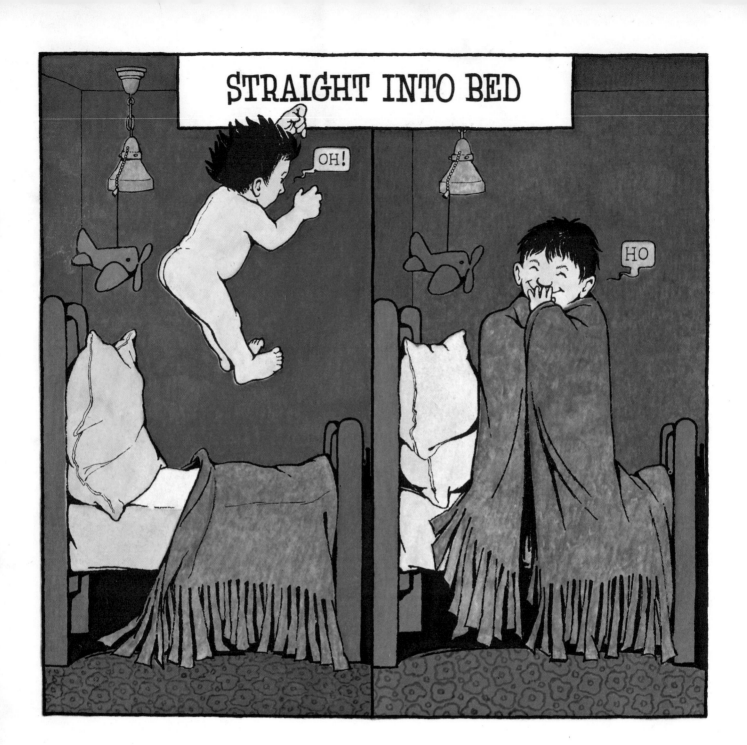